# A TALE FOR

## Easter

by

## Tasha Tudor

ALADDIN PAPERBACKS

NEW YORK   LONDON   TORONTO   SYDNEY   SINGAPORE

Dearest
Mary Ann,

Happy Easter
2012

Love,
Aunt Jacque'
Uncle Tom

First Aladdin Paperbacks edition February 2004

ALADDIN PAPERBACKS
An imprint of Simon & Schuster
Children's Publishing Division
1230 Avenue of the Americas
New York, NY 10020

Also available in a Simon & Schuster Books for Young Readers hardcover edition.
Designed by Heather Wood
The text of this book was set in Didot Roman Oldstyle. The illustrations were rendered in watercolor.

Manufactured in China
4 6 8 10 9 7 5
0411 SCP
The Library of Congress has cataloged the hardcover edition as follows:
Tudor, Tasha
A tale for Easter / by Tasha Tudor.
p. cm.
Summary: While awaiting the arrival of Easter, a child dreams of rabbits with shining eyes,
little lambs, Easter ducklings, and other wonderful surprises.
ISBN 0-689-82844-6 (hc.)
[1. Easter—Fiction. 2. Animals—Fiction.] I. Title.
PZ7.T8228 Tal 2001 [E]—dc21 99-462167
ISBN 978-0-689-86694-4 (Aladdin pbk.)

To
LITTLE ANN NEWELL

You can never tell
what might happen on Easter.

You're not always sure when it is coming,
even though you go to Sunday school.

You can guess it is near

when Mama makes you stand still
while she fits a new dress on you.

But it is only when Good Friday comes,
and you have hot cross buns for tea,

that you know for certain
Easter will be the day after tomorrow.

On Saturday you go
and ask the chickens

to lay you plenty of Easter eggs.

If you have been very good
the whole year through,

the night before Easter
you will dream the loveliest dreams.

One will be about a wee fawn,

who makes you as light as thistledown
and takes you on her back and
gallops through the woods and fields.

She shows you rabbits

smoothing their sleek coats
for Easter morning.

And mice with beady eyes

and shining whiskers.

Little lambs, too,

in fields of buttercups.

And Easter ducklings

swimming among the lily pads.

If you have been especially good
and done nearly everything you have been told,

she will take you up, up,
over the misty moisty clouds,
where the bluebirds dye their feathers,
and the robins find the color for their eggs.

But this is only if you have been good

and can find the stardust on daffodils
with your eyes tight shut.

And when you wake up in the morning

there isn't any fawn at all,
and you are just you again.
But often there are colored eggs in your shoes
or in your best bonnet.

Or a basket of ducklings
beside your bowl of porridge.

There might even be a bunny
in Grandma's rocking chair.

You can never really tell,
for anything might happen
on Easter.